ANNE AND GRAN

Jean Watson

Illustrated by Toni Goffe

VICTOR BOOKS

A DIVISION OF SCRIPTURE PRESS PUBLICATIONS INC.
USA CANADA ENGLAND

Anne was down in the dumps. She had been sick and indoors for a whole week. And now Mom was going shopping without her.

But she cheered up a bit when Gran arrived and said, "Never mind. While your mom's out, we can go on one of our expeditions."

Anne and her Gran were great friends. Gran lived down the road and Anne dropped by to see her most days. Sometimes they had snacks together. Sometimes they went for walks together. Gran never minded stopping to watch a snail uncoil or smell leaves or peep under stones.

Sometimes they played games together. One of their favorite games was "Let's pretend." Sometimes they told each other jokes and laughed. Sometimes they talked about feeling scared and growing up and God.

After Mom had gone, Gran said, "Now, where shall we go? You choose."

"Africa!" said Anne. So they put on safari hats and jackets. Then, carrying peanut butter sandwiches, they set off.

First they came to swampy country. Anne said, "Ssh!" and pointed to what looked like a long piece of bark. But she and Gran knew it was a very long snout.

"I hope it isn't hungry!" said Anne as they tiptoed past.

Then they came to rocky country.

"Look!" whispered Anne. On one of the rocks was something that looked like a black cat. But Anne and Gran were not fooled.

"I'm glad it's asleep," Anne said as they tiptoed past.

Then they came to wooded country.

"Aha!" said Anne, pointing to what looked like long, dangling branches. But Anne and Gran knew that they were animal trunks.

"Shall we take a photo?" asked Anne.
"Too close," said Gran. "Better keep going."

They went further into the wooded country. Anne stopped and pointed to what looked like two tall, smooth, mottled tree trunks. But she and Gran knew that they were two very long necks.

"Do you think they've seen us?" asked Anne.

"No," said Gran. "They go to sleep standing up. Can you imagine?"

"No, I can't!" said Anne.

Afterward, they went to some sandy country.

"Let's dig for buried treasure," said Anne. So they sat and talked and dug. Anne dug up something that looked like a ball. But she and Gran knew it was an egg.

"Perhaps it's a snake's egg," said Gran. "They sometimes hide their eggs in sand."

"Better bury it again, quick!" said Anne. So they did.

"Shall we see what's over the next hill?" asked Anne.

"All right," said Gran. So they did. Lying down below them was what looked like the spotted dog from next door. Anne pointed and said, "Good thing it's asleep."

But it wasn't. It lept to its feet and ran, making a loud barking, howling noise. That was when Anne and Gran noticed where the panther had gone.

But the chase didn't last long because the panther was up and over the hill again in a flash and the cheetah flopped down exhausted.

A bit later, Anne and Gran came to some grassy country and flopped down too.

"These sandwiches are yummy," said Anne. Then Gran pointed to what looked like a couple of squirrels in some trees nearby.

"Their tails are like ropes," said Anne as she and
Gran looked up into the branches overhead.

Then Anne gave a great big yawn and Gran said,
"Time to safari back home for a nap, don't you
think?"

When Anne was in bed, Gran said, "You look much better—not down in the dumps at all. Amazing what a bit of fresh air and a good imagination can do."

"Do you really think I've got a good imagination, Gran?" asked Anne.

"No doubt about it," said Gran.

"I'm glad," said Anne.

"So am I," said Gran. "It's one of God's great gifts to you, along with your strong body, which is helping you to get better again."

"And along with a Gran who's the best pretender in the world," said Anne, giving Gran a bear hug. A few minutes later she was happily asleep.

1 2 3 4 5 6 7 8 9 10 Printing/Year 99 98 97 96 95

Published in the United States by Victor Books / SP Publications Inc.,
Wheaton, Illinois.
Printed in Singapore.

ISBN: 1-56476-365-X